Elfin-Glades

Elfin-Glades

4

9

7

Elfin

3

Elfin-Glades

For Nyela Asad, because
this story really happened
to her Aunt Claire,
with love
—P.D.E.

For Caoilfhionn and Megan
—M.L.F.

Dear Tooth Fairy
Text copyright © 2003 by Pamela Duncan Edwards
Illustrations copyright © 2003 by Marie-Louise Fitzpatrick
Manufactured in China. All rights reserved.
www.harperchildrens.com

Library of Congress Cataloging-in-Publication Data

Edwards, Pamela Duncan.
    Dear Tooth Fairy / by Pamela Duncan Edwards ; illustrated by Marie-Louise
Fitzpatrick.
        p.   cm.
    Summary: In a series of letters, six-year-old Claire and the Tooth Fairy discuss the
important matter of her first loose tooth and when it is going to fall out.
    ISBN 0-06-623972-9 — ISBN 0-06-623973-7 (lib. bdg.)
    [1. Tooth Fairy—Fiction. 2. Teeth—Fiction. 3. Letters—Fiction.] I. Fitzpatrick,
Marie-Louise, ill. II. Title.
PZ7. E26365bDe 2003   2002007641
[E]—dc21   CIP
                                                                            AC

Typography by Jeanne L. Hogle
5 6 7 8 9 10
❖
First Edition

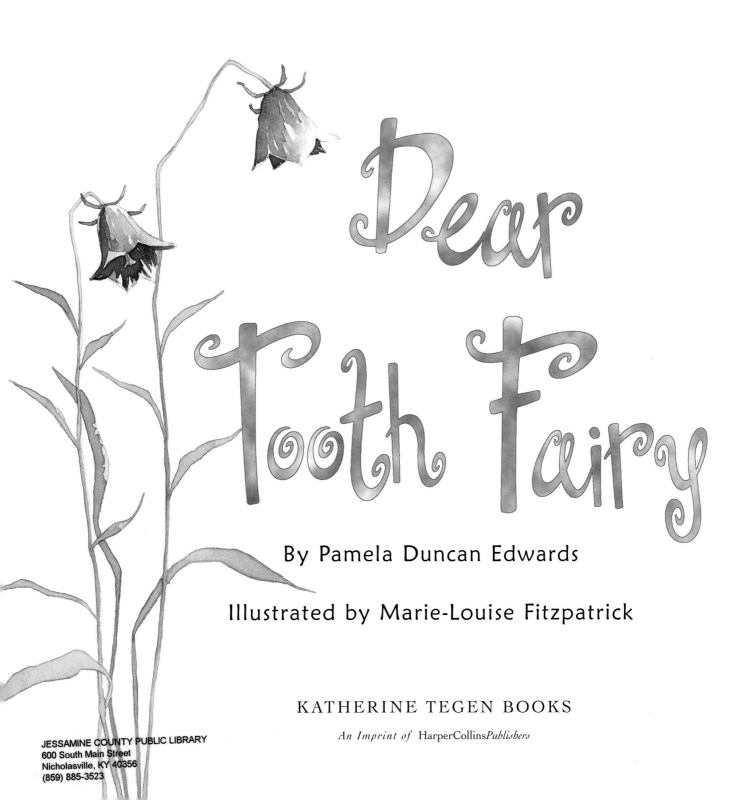

Dear Tooth Fairy

By Pamela Duncan Edwards

Illustrated by Marie-Louise Fitzpatrick

KATHERINE TEGEN BOOKS

An Imprint of HarperCollins*Publishers*

Dear Tooth Fairy,

    Last week it was my birthday. I was six, but I don't have even one wobbly tooth yet. I'm worried.

                        Yours sincerely,
                        Claire

Dear Tooth Fairy,

   Did you get the letter I sent you three days ago?
I told my friend Amanda about writing to you.
She asked if I could mention her because she doesn't
have any wobbly teeth either. But that's okay because
Amanda is much younger than me. She isn't six for
another four weeks.

                    Yours sincerely,
                    Claire

Dear Tooth Fairy,

Today our teacher told Jimmy Clarke to stop fiddling with his wobbly tooth. Jimmy Clarke said he wasn't fiddling with his wobbly tooth—he was fiddling with his TWO wobbly teeth.

Amanda and I thought Jimmy Clarke was a big bragger, so we didn't play with him on the playground.

Yours sincerely,
Claire

Dear Tooth Fairy,

My friend Amanda and I went to visit my grandma after school. Grandma said tooth fairies get busy at this time of the year and we'd have to be patient and wait our turn.

Grandma didn't think Jimmy Clarke was bragging when he told us about his two wobbly teeth. She said we should be glad for him. So we're going to ask him to Amanda's birthday party.

Yours sincerely,
Claire

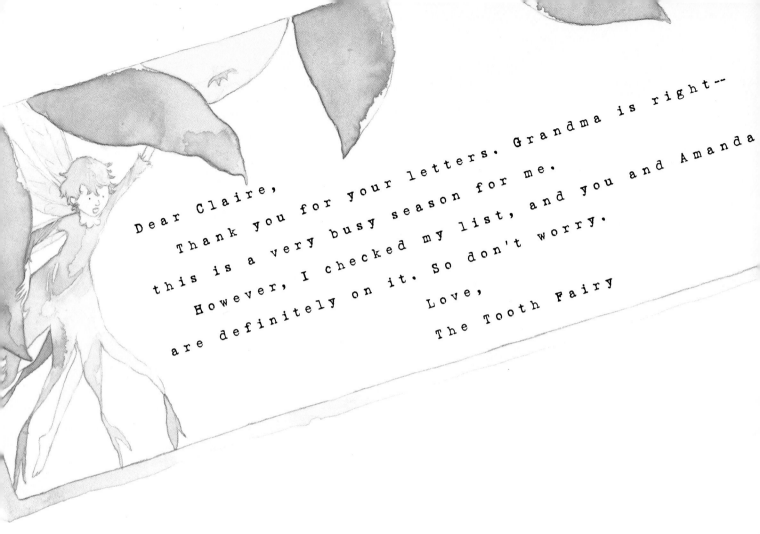

Dear Claire,

Thank you for your letters. Grandma is right-- this is a very busy season for me.

However, I checked my list, and you and Amanda are definitely on it. So don't worry.

Love,
The Tooth Fairy

Dear Tooth Fairy,

My friend Amanda and I jumped up and down and cheered when we got your letter.
Did I tell you that I am already six?

Love,
Claire

Dear Claire,

I know it's hard to believe, but I have people on my list who are almost seven, and they still don't have wobbly teeth. Wobbly teeth like to be hurried. They wobble when they're ready.

You are taking care of your teeth, aren't you? I hope you are brushing them twice a day, because I really like to collect shiny white teeth.

Love,
The Tooth Fairy

Dear Tooth Fairy,

Everyone from our class came to Amanda's party.
We played all these party games, and it was great. Jimmy
Clarke wobbled his two teeth and made Amanda's mom
laugh.

But the best news of all is, I THINK I HAVE A WOBBLY
TOOTH AT LAST! I was eating a piece of birthday cake,
and I'm sure my front tooth moved.

Amanda was sad at first, but I told her not to worry—
when she's as old as me, she'll get a wobbly tooth, too.

Love,
Claire

Dear Claire,
I told you so!

Love,
The Tooth Fairy

Dear Tooth Fairy,

It's amazing! Amanda and I are twins! She's got
a wobbly tooth, too.

Grandma took us out to celebrate. Amanda
had butterscotch ice cream and I had chocolate.
Grandma had mint. I hate mint. Except mint
toothpaste is okay, I suppose.

Amanda says to tell you that we brushed our
teeth after the ice cream. We want our teeth to be
white and shiny for you.

Love,
Claire

Dear Claire,

My favorite ice cream is bubble gum. Did you know you can get bubble-gum-flavor toothpaste? In fact, toothpaste comes in lots of different flavors, just like ice cream.

Love,

The Tooth Fairy

Dear Tooth Fairy,

I'm sorry I haven't written for a long time, but yesterday was Halloween, and Amanda and I have been planning our costumes.

Amanda went as a tooth, and I went as you! We told Jimmy Clarke he should go as a tube of toothpaste, but he said that was silly. He went as a pirate instead.

Grandma gave us little boxes to put our teeth in when they fall out. She gave one to Jimmy Clarke, too, even though he was only dressed up as a pirate.

Love,
Claire

Dear Claire,

I'm looking forward to seeing your little tooth boxes. Sometimes a tooth gets lost under the pillows, and it takes me a long time to find it.

Love,
The Tooth Fairy

Dear Tooth Fairy,

I've had this wobbly tooth for absolutely ages. Do you think it's ever going to come out?

Love,
Claire

Dear Tooth Fairy,

Don't bother to read my last letter because MY WOBBLY TOOTH CAME OUT TODAY! I screamed and made everyone jump. But our teacher didn't mind. She said she was pleased and put my name on the Tooth Chart.

Jimmy Clarke was a bit mad because he's had two wobbly teeth for so long. He said, "Yuck, that's gross," when my gum was bleeding. But I told him I bet he'll be the first boy to get on the Tooth Chart.

Love,
Claire

P.S. My tooth will be on the table by my bed. Could you leave the little box behind? I'll need it for my next tooth.

Dear Claire,

I'm pleased you took such good care of your tooth. It's really white and shiny. I'm going to use it for my own special fairy carriage.

Love,
The Tooth Fairy

Dear Tooth Fairy,

Thank you for leaving me the dollar for my tooth. The fairies must have so many carriages. I bet you have traffic jams sometimes.

By the way, I don't want to rush you, but I'm wondering—WHEN DO YOU THINK I'LL GET MY NEXT WOBBLY TOOTH?

Love,
Claire

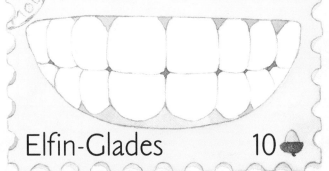

5 🌰

Elfin-Glades 10 🌰

8 🌰

Elfin-Glades 6 🌰

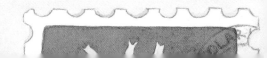